ABOUT THE AUTHOR

David Melling was born in Oxford.
His first book was shortlisted for the Smarties
Book Award and The Kiss that Missed was
shortlisted for the Kate Greenaway Award.
He is married and lives with his wife
and children in Oxfordshire.

For more information, go to:
www.davidmelling.co.uk

Look

out for

all the

GOBLINS

books:

Stone Goblins
Tree Goblins
Puddle Goblins
Shadow Goblins

tree GOBLINS

David Melling

Hodder
Children's
Books

A division of Hachette Children's Books

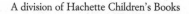

Printed and bound in Germany by GGP Media GmbH, Pößneck

The paper used in this book is a natural recyclable product made from wood
grown in sustainable forests. The hard coverboard is recycled.

Hodder Children's Books
A division of Hachette Children's Books
338 Euston Road, London NW1 3BH
An Hachette Livre UK Company

Fingerprints by Monika and Luka Melling

For Rachel Wade

inside Wandering Wood

We all like being looked after – a nice cosy feeling, I think you'll agree.

Now imagine being looked after by someone taller than the tallest giant, standing on tiptoes in high-heeled boots, tottering along on stilts, with the hug of ten big bears and the smell of a wet autumn morning.

Well, that's what it feels like for a Tree Goblin living in a tree. Makes you want to go for a stroll in the woods ... don't you think?

Introducing the Tree Goblins

Butterfingers

Kind but clumsy. Always standing up

at the wrong moment, tipping

Mildew out of the tree.

Mildew

Grumpy, because she is always being dropped
by **Butterfingers**, but a very patient goblin.
She was the first female goblin to try wearing a
large conker shell instead of clothes (helps
to protect her when she falls). Most
female goblins now do the same.

Egglets

Tree Goblins lay two to three eggs (or 'pods') which look exactly like the shell of a horse chestnut, or conker. They hatch quickly, but remain in their shells, changing for bigger ones as they grow, like a hermit crab. Later they keep one half and wear it as a cap. Can speak almost immediately. Love to argue.

Drips

A bit of a loner. Helpful and brave.

Very inventive. His best invention

is Sock-Sucking.

Two-Conks

A horse chestnut tree, host to Butterfingers
and Mildew. So called because his large
nose looks a bit like two noses.
(Conk is another word for nose!)

Rumble-Bark

An elderly tree. Sometimes shakes her bark
and purrs like a cat, a low rumbling sound,
which is how she got her name.

Snootle-pig

They are nosy and nasty
(ruthless hunters), but have terrible
memories. They make fish look
very clever.

Wood Owl

A night bird foolish
enough, in this story,
to try and pinch
Tree-Goblin eggs.

Ground-bat

Small woodland creature. Hunts
by groping around in the hope of
catching something. Very blind,
very nervous, very silly.

A FEW FACTS ABOUT TREE GOBLINS

 **CHARACTERISTICS**

a) Shy.

b) But can be aggressive if surprised.

Tip No 1: **NEVER** poke a Tree Goblin.

c) Very well camouflaged,
making them difficult to see.

Behind one of these leaves is a Tree Goblin –
can you guess which one? (Actually, that doesn't
count, this Tree Goblin's a plonk.)

Note: if a male goblin is too well camouflaged, a passing bird may mistake him for a spare nest. All he can do is wait until the bird is finished and then try to start his own family again.

FAMILY TREES

A tree host is happy to have a collection of Tree Goblins living in its branches. The goblins look after the tree, pruning its leaves, wiping its nose and giving it a little tickle if it's feeling a bit sad. The tree, in return, will protect the goblins from larger creatures, and carry them great distances in a short time if needed.

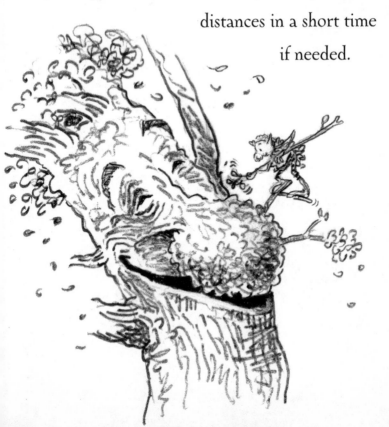

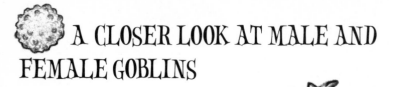 A CLOSER LOOK AT MALE AND FEMALE GOBLINS

The male builds a nest to attract a female. If he succeeds, he has to piggyback the nest, the eggs and the female day and night.

While he is having a little rest, let's take a quick look at some of a Tree Goblin's more important bits.

Nose – A female hugs her eggs close to her face. Her nose looks just like an egg. If something is stupid enough to try and steal an egg, there is a fair chance they will pick her nose.

Tip No 2: **NEVER** pick a Tree Goblin's nose.

Hands – Strong fingers for gripping and climbing.

Feet – Some Tree Goblins have monkey feet i.e. a foot-thumb! A good thumb will attract a female. It tells her that her mate is sensible and really good at climbing.

WANDERING WOOD

Trees like to travel in groups. That is to say, the trees move and the woodland creatures have to follow.

It takes a while for some of the creatures to get used to this. Going to bed in the comfortable surroundings of the wood, they can wake to a cruel whipping wind, all alone, in a bleak wilderness.

SOCK-SUCKING

Drips has discovered a time-saving way to drink water at any time of the day or night – without having to climb in and out of a tree in search of it. The answer is – a sock. He found an old sock* in a puddle one day and sucked the water from it. It was delicious! He soaked it again like a sponge, and decided to take it with him – it lasted all day.

He keeps the soggy sock tied to his body with string and strap. When his trousers start to dry, he knows it's time for a re-soak.

No one knows who the sock belongs to, whether it is man, beast or very large goblin.

PLONKERS WITH CONKERS

An argument can be settled by playing conkers.

Official Conker Kit: one conker (per player),

conker socks (no one really knows why).

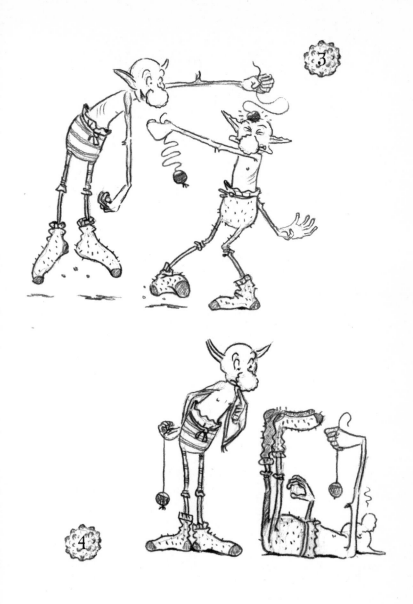

RULES: ER, SEE IF YOU CAN WORK IT OUT.

Contents

The Story Begins ...

A small floppy sock peeped out from the hollow of an oak tree and sniffed the air. The sun had not long set on a rain-sodden day, and until the moon came out, the trees of Wandering Wood looked like black strips of torn paper.

Humming a well-known goblin jig, the sock clambered down his tree to fuss among the leaves and roots.

In truth, it was not a sock, so much as a sock-wearing Tree Goblin. His name was Drips and he was looking for rain puddles.

Finding one, he loosened his belt and draped the sock into the puddle. He closed his eyes and smiled happily. For the next ten minutes the sock would slowly soak up the water like a sponge. Then he could return to his hollow and think about making a nice warm cup of toenail tea.

Suddenly something heavy came crashing down from the tree, only just missing him. It was followed seconds later by a slightly smaller something.

Drips stopped humming and held his breath. He waited for the trailing leaves to settle before daring to take a peek. Were they friend or foe?

He decided to pretend not to be there. Perhaps they'd go away.

OOPS!

"**Of all the silly, nitwitted, knobbly-nosed, gobblede-gooked plonks I've ever come across, YOU, Mr Butterfingers, take the biscuit!**"

It was Mildew who'd just fallen out of the tree. She lay sprawled on the ground, still clutching her eggs.

Sitting up, she arranged the eggs carefully next to her, and began picking out bits of twig from some of the more uncomfortable places.

"What happened?" came a voice, groggy and

3

muffled with leaves.

"I would have thought," said Mildew, "that was obvious."

Butterfingers went quiet and tried to think.

Whenever they fell out of the tree, it always took him a few moments to rewind his memory and work out exactly how it had happened. He closed his eyes and this is what he saw:

Butterfingers, a little hungry, stands up to reach a beetle.

4

Mildew falls out.

Butterfingers tries to catch her on her way down.

He loses his balance and tumbles after her.

Mildew lands first, with a bounce.

Followed by Butterfingers.

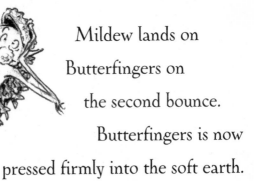

Mildew lands on Butterfingers on the second bounce.

Butterfingers is now pressed firmly into the soft earth.

Mildew (finally) stops bouncing.

"My fault, then," said Butterfingers slowly.
"Umm … sorry!"

But Mildew wasn't listening. She was watching
two twiglet-thin fingers peeking out from one of
the eggs.

"They're hatching, *already!*" she said, squeaking
with excitement. Butterfingers groped his way

towards her, still a little dizzy. Sure enough two of the three eggs were wriggling around inside their soft shells like bats in a bag.

"Don't forget," said Butterfingers, "I get to choose the boys' names, and you can choose the girls'."

"But we won't know what they are until they leave their pods, and they won't do that until who *knows* when!"

"So what are we going to do?" asked Butterfingers.

"Why, give them sensible boy or girl names, like Mucus or Squelch or Dollop," said Mildew.

"Dollop?" said Butterfingers, "That's a bit *soft*, isn't it? Next you'll be dressing them up in little gloves and booties and speaking to them in silly made-up voices."

"I don't know what you mean," sniffed Mildew. "Anyway, we'd better get off the ground before a snootle-pig smells us."

"And we must show Two-Conks, of course," said Butterfingers. All Tree Goblins like to introduce their newly hatched eggs to their host tree.

They stood up and brushed themselves down.

"Oh, and by the way," said Mildew, holding up a finger, "drop me like that again and I'll flick my stick! Understand?"

Butterfingers blinked. "Yes, my sweet."

OOPS! (again)

"**A**nd have you thought of any names yet?"
asked Two-Conks. He was holding up the
wriggling eggs between his twiggy fingers.

"None that would make you smile," muttered Butterfingers.

"We're still thinking about it," said Mildew, giving Butterfingers a sharp look.

"My mother's family had some lovely names," said Two-Conks thoughtfully. "How about Root-Finger, or Timber-Chips, or Leaf-Ear?"

"Mmm," said Mildew politely. "Something to think about, certainly!"

When the two Tree Goblins finally reached their favourite branch, Mildew climbed into the nest on Butterfingers' back and cuddled her eggs. It was usual for a male Tree Goblin to do all the carrying, but it always took Mildew a little time after a fall to feel completely comfortable again.

Butterfingers is a good Tree Goblin, she thought. He's just a bit of a plonk when it comes to standing up without thinking.

She snuggled a little deeper into the warm mossy leaves. She might as well rest now. Tomorrow was going to be a busy day. She gave the eggs a little squeeze and closed her eyes. Butterfingers was already asleep, his right leg twitching.

Butterfingers woke to the sound of arguing. He looked up at the moon and guessed it was the middle of the night.

"But if you poke her *there* she's not going to like it, is she?" he heard Mildew say.

There was a muffled reply. Butterfingers realised that his egglets were talking already! He felt a glow of pride.

Mildew continued, "I know she shouldn't have done that, but we can clean it up in the morning. And don't worry, the smell will soon go away."

Butterfingers closed his eyes quickly and tried very hard to go back to sleep. But a foot surprised him with a kick. It was Mildew, of course. She had managed to put her foot through the lining of the nest.

"You all right up there?" Butterfingers squeaked.

"Oh, how nice of you to join us," snipped Mildew. "This lot have been awake all night – I haven't had a wink yet. You take them for a bit, while I clear this mess up!"

A long stick appeared over the rim of the nest, the three wriggling eggs attached to it. Butterfingers scratched his head.

"Before you hurt yourself thinking," said Mildew, "I've tied the eggs to the stick – makes them easier to carry."

"Ah!" said Butterfingers.

He took the stick and smiled. "Goo-goo ga-ga?" he cooed.

The wriggling stopped.

"Was that you?" came a voice from one of the eggs.

"Don't be a plonk – who speaks like that?" replied the second egg.

"Talking of plonks," said the third, "who's that idiot out there looking at us?"

Butterfingers coughed.

"Daddy!" they all squealed at once. "You *smell* funny."

"Why, thank you – what a lovely thing to say," said Butterfingers. He jiggled them around a bit, until one of them was sick.

"Who's a clever goblin then," cooed Butterfingers, looking down. "Goodness, what a lot – and from such a little one! Now let me just wipe that up for you, shall I? And, um … don't tell your mother. She would be cross if she knew she'd missed you doing that for the first time."

When he had finished, the egglets yawned, one after the other.

"I know," suggested Butterfingers, "how about a quick story and then time for a snoozle?"

"Yes all right, a story about a plonky baby Tree Goblin what is sick all over her sister," said the first egg.

"No, how about a baby Tree Goblin that looks like a caterpillar's bottom!" replied the second.

"Or about a *nice* baby Tree Goblin who has two silly sisters that can't stop quarrelling," squealed the third.

A crabby voice interrupted the story before it began. "Time for bed, my little ones. Pass them up, would you, Butterfingers?"

"Yes, my petal, they're just com—"

"No, WAIT!" cried Mildew. "DON'T STAND UP!"

But it was too late.

Butterfingers just managed to catch the look of utter disbelief on Mildew's face as she toppled over the side of the nest.

"Try not to land on your head," he heard himself call out. Mildew seemed to be saying something as she shrank in size, but he didn't catch it.

A small cloud of exploding leaves, far below, told him when she landed. Another two smaller clouds showed her bounces, and then silence.

"Are you all right?" Butterfingers ventured.

Moments passed, then a voice, cold and sharp as broken ice, found its way up to him. She wouldn't let him forget this one, he thought.

"Coming, my sweet!" he called.

The Snatch

B y the time he was halfway down the tree,
Butterfingers could hear Mildew shouting
at him from the ground.

"The eggs! Have you got the
eggs?"

Butterfingers thought for a minute before
realising she meant for him to check the
nest.

"I'll check the nest," he nodded.

Mildew suddenly squealed up to him, waving
her hands frantically, "NO, WAIT! – DON'T
STAND UP!"

Butterfingers stood up.

"Oops!" was all he managed to say as he pitched the remaining members of his family into the chilly night.

Butterfingers hurried down. He thought of jumping straight after the eggs – he'd had higher falls and lived! – but thought better of it. If he landed on Mildew …

Mildew, meanwhile, had begun climbing *up*. She was screaming, and Butterfingers thought it was at him. But then he noticed her pointing at something. Butterfingers followed her gaze along a thin branch and there, dangling on a single twig, were the three eggs!

Both Tree Goblins scrambled towards the egglets as fast as they could. But the thin branch wasn't strong enough for both of them. It snapped.

Once again
Butterfingers, Mildew
and the eggs were
airborne … but almost
immediately, Butterfingers'
trousers were caught on
another branch.
Somehow he
managed to
grab hold
of Mildew,
who in turn had got hold of
the eggs. And there they
hung, like a string of
sausages!

"Can this night *possibly* get
any worse?" mumbled Mildew.

20

It was Butterfingers, of course, who happened to sneeze. And when he did, he shook … so Mildew shook … and the eggs just somehow slipped from her grasp. But once again, they managed to tangle themselves on yet another branch, just out of reach.

Well, Butterfingers and Mildew wasted no time in righting themselves, then scrambled frantically after the eggs before anything else happened.

Now, Tree Goblins are excellent climbers. They have long thin fingers which are very strong, perfect for gripping Two-Conks' bark. But their fingers are so good at working their way into the rough folds of the bark that sometimes, as they scuttle around, it is quite ticklish for the tree.

If Two-Conks had been awake, he would most probably have helped gather them all together safely. Unfortunately, it was the middle of the night and he was asleep. And no matter how hard you try, it's almost impossible to wake a sleeping tree, so deep and far away are their dreams.

But the sudden excitement of the Tree Goblins, with their scrambling fingers and toes, was enough to stir Two-Conks – who was very ticklish. His favourite dream about The Giant of Snow-Tree Wood was suddenly feeling more real, with its feather-light snowflakes fluttering around his sensitive tummy bark! He snorted a series of sleepy giggles.

The Tree Goblins were inches away from their eggs when Two-Conks' giggles became louder and he began to wriggle and twist in his sleep.

It was enough to dislodge the eggs. They fell.

"Weeeee!" said the baby goblins, peeking out from their shells.

They bounced off the head of a soggy sock – it was Drips, who squeaked and fell over.

Butterfingers and Mildew let out a sigh of relief when they saw the eggs' fall cushioned by the sock. But before the eggs could bounce for a second time, a wood owl dropped out of the shadows. She snatched the eggs in her talons and flew up and away!

"NOOOOOOOOOOO!"
screeched Mildew.

The wood owl looked down at Butterfingers and Mildew as she flew. But, like the ground below her, their screams gradually faded away.

A Plonk Too Far

Mildew was pressed nose to nose with Butterfingers. As Mildew's yellow face bubbled with anger, Butterfingers thought how much it looked like boiling custard. He was also amazed at how long her sentences could last without her actually taking a breath.

"I mean, what is it with you and the standing up? You know the standing up is a no-no when you've got your nest on! DON'T... STAND... UP! How many more times..?"

The voice of another Tree Goblin floated gently down from a neighbouring tree.

"Could you two keep quiet down there, only, it *is* the middle of the night and my eggs need their beauty sleep."

Mildew felt the need to hit something.

Five minutes later, Mildew was back in the branches. Two-Conks had finally woken up and she'd decided to ask him what to do.

Meanwhile, down on the ground, Butterfingers lay unconscious among the leaves, a hand-shaped bruise glowing in the moonlight. It was the best half hour's rest he would get that night.

The Search Begins

N ow Two-Conks, at 458 years old, wasn't the oldest tree in Wandering Wood. But he *knew* things, and he had the wrinkles to prove it. The Tree Goblins would always go to him when they had a problem, however small.

When Mildew had finished telling Two-Conks what had happened, he rumbled his most thoughtful of noises!

Trees, by their very nature, are slow creatures. For them there is little need for hurrying. They move and talk at their own pace and in their own time. It is not unusual for a tree to stand still and think for years.

But whether moving or standing still, they love talking to each other.

"Don't worry, my little goblins. Here in Wandering Wood our eyes may be small, but our leaves are many. And our leaves help us see, hear and feel."

"Do you really think you can help us?" said Butterfingers. He'd managed to find his way back up, despite the headache.

Two-Conks smiled, his eyes disappearing for a moment in the rippled lines of bark.

Now, there are many ways of talking without the use of words, and trees are particularly good at it. Leaves, the very lifeline of any wood, are used the way we send letters.

29

Two-Conks shivered a little, like a bird ruffling its feathers, and whispered something in the sounds of the summer winds. Then he raised a branch high into the air and, still whispering, he shook the leaves free, blowing as he did so.

The leaves chattered to each other excitedly and floated into the wood, spreading the news about the egglets as they went. The leaves from other trees listened and shook, like waving flags. Some of these, too, fell on to the breeze and carried the news further and deeper into the wood.

Still more leaves joined in, dancing in all directions. The Tree Goblins looked on in wonder. They had never seen this before – it was snowing leaves!

"We must wait a while, little goblins," said

Two-Conks. "But news of your eggs will reach us soon. Be patient."

The Tree Goblins nodded.

"Perhaps, while we wait, you can have a word with that thing down there," Two-Conks continued.

Butterfingers and Mildew followed his pointing twig.

"A *sock*?"

"Indeed!" said Two-Conks. "No ordinary sock, mind. It's another Tree Goblin, Drips. Nice fellow: got a thing about puddles, but a good little worker – he'll help you if he can. He moved in last week. I've been meaning to introduce you, only you've been busy with your eggs and—" He stopped when he saw Mildew's worried face.

"Anyway, you speak to him. There's not many that notice him when he's working the puddles – he might have seen something. Go on, give him a try. I'll keep talking with the leaves."

The Wood Owl

The wood owl had been quite pleased with her catch. She wasn't quite sure what she had picked up in her talons, but it looked like food so she'd decided to nab it.

But now she was feeling very uncomfortable. The problem was that the very *trees* in this strange and enchanted wood seemed to be talking to each other. And if that wasn't bad enough, they appeared to be talking about *her*!

She was new to these woods and didn't like them at all. Having tried to settle in a number of trees, each of which seemed to do its very best to shoo her away, she had finally chanced upon an ideal spot:

an ancient wall of stone. Who knows why it was there – Stone Goblins are known to build up walls for reasons unknown. (Truth be told, if you asked a whole bunch of them one at a time they'd probably shrug, then go about building another one.)

The wood owl made her way there now, keen to take a look at exactly what she had and how best to eat it.

She landed clumsily. The eggs felt as though they were moving.

She took a closer look. They *were* moving! Little muffled voices, sharp yellow eyes, long thin pointy fingers, and she knew – they were *Tree-Goblin* eggs!

That explained why she had felt so unwelcome in this strange wood. Her feathers prickled.

Trees will tolerate birds, but not if they attack their goblins.

There was only one thing to do. She took off again, flew a short way from the wall and dropped the egglets. Then instead of returning to the wall she decided to fly away, far away, out of Wandering Wood and to a place where trees were trees and stayed good and still – and didn't whisper about her!

Soon her silent shadow melted into the night and she was gone.

Chapter Seven

Drips

When they reached the sock that was Drips, Butterfingers and Mildew were surprised to hear that it was *humming*. Butterfingers coughed politely and the humming stopped.

They waited a full minute, Butterfingers passing the time by counting the drops coming from the sock. Then he took a step closer. Using thumb and forefinger, he lifted the frayed edge of the sock and smiled.

"Er, you'll be Drips – that right?"

Drips blinked his surprise. It very much looked as though he had been discovered. He was used to all the creatures of Wandering Wood – and

that included other Tree Goblins – passing him
by without a second glance. And if anything did
want to take a closer look, one whiff of wet sock
was usually enough to change their minds. Yet
here were two Tree Goblins looking at him.

Most unsettling, he thought.
But when Butterfingers and
Mildew explained what
had happened, and how
Two-Conks had suggested
they talk to him, he felt
much better. It had actually
been a while since he'd spoken to
another Tree Goblin and it was a
nice change.

"Well, now that you're
asking," he said, "it's been
the most amazing night. You'll never believe
what's been happening here, honest you
wouldn't!"

"What have you seen?" asked Mildew,
rubbing her arms nervously.

"Well, I came down here my usual time, and got myself all comfy like, with my puddle and my sock. When all of a sudden these terrible creatures come crashing down around me – beasts of the night for sure! They was groaning and growling, making a right hullabaloo – honest, it was all I could do not to run, I was that scared!"

"So what did you do?" asked Butterfingers, eyes wide. He had no idea that Drips was talking about the moment he and Mildew had fallen out of Two-Conks, earlier that night.

"I froze, didn't I. If I don't move, things don't see me. And smelling the way I does, things don't *want* to come near me."

"I see," said Butterfingers. He thought it was quite a nice smell – sort of cold, grey bathwater with onions.

"Oh yes," continued Drips, "I just melt into the background. Cunning as a fox and twice as smelly, that's me!"

"You got that right," mumbled Mildew.

She looked at Butterfingers who was sniffing Drips, and gave him a kick. "Can we get back to the main point here? We're trying to find out if you know anything about the wood owl that's taken our eggs. You know, where it roosts, something like that?"

"Well, I did see it, as it happens. Don't get many wood owls round these parts, as I'm sure you know. I've heard Rumble-Bark talking about having a bit of trouble with one – scaring off her goblins."

"Rumble-Bark?" said Mildew. "Two-Conks mentioned her name before. Quick, let's go and have another word. I'm sure he'll take us to see her."

"Thanks for your help, Drips," Butterfingers called as they turned to go.

"Well, actually," said Drips, "I was thinking of coming with you. I'm all socked up and ready to go. Maybe I can help – the more the merrier, right?"

So they all made their way up the trunk.

As they climbed, Butterfingers spoke to Drips. "This, er … *sock* arrangement … you, um, carry it around all day, do you?"

"Absolutely!" grinned Drips. "It's my own invention – do you like it? Saves no end of climbing up and down a tree all day long looking for something to drink. I just suck the sock any time I'm thirsty."

"Really?"

"Absolutely! Lasts the whole day sometimes, unless I get the sweats from working. But that never happens!" said Drips, slapping his knee in a fit of giggles. He stopped suddenly, looking thoughtfully at Butterfingers. "Mind you, what with that load on your back, you must get the sweats something awful – you should give it a go."

Butterfingers was already thinking about it. And the more he thought, the better he liked the idea of a nice damp *sock* to keep him cool.

Chapter Eight

The Ground-Bat

"Weeeeeeeeeeeeeeeee!" cried the Tree-Goblin eggs when the wood owl let them go.

Most Tree-Goblin eggs spend their life hanging about in trees. But the three egglets had spent the best part of the night flying and bouncing their

way around Wandering Wood.

It was great fun!

"Last one to bounce is an egg-head!" said one.

"First one to bounce *twice* is an egg-leg," said another.

"What's an egg-*leg*?" asked the third.

"Don't know, but we're going to find out in a minute! Weeeeeeeeeeeeeeeeeee!"

Moments away from a rather nice surprise, a ground-bat was fumbling his way through the undergrowth. He had been looking for a meal all night long, and was getting a little agitated. There was only about an hour before sunrise and he'd found nothing.

Ground-bats are small, nervous creatures and for good reason. They are totally blind and must therefore grope their way through the black and puzzling world that is Wandering Wood, with all its dangers, large and small. They hunt with their arms outstretched, waving their hands about in a flappy kind of way.

If they do bump into anything edible (usually by accident), then they must grab hold of it quickly. If they don't, the potential victim has an annoying habit of running away.

You will not be surprised to learn that ground-bats are rubbish at hunting. And they are nervous, of course, because by stumbling around the way they do, the chances of eating or being eaten are worryingly equal.

So, back to this nice surprise. Suddenly, and without warning, three large Tree-Goblin eggs came crashing down, snapping the twig and so allowing them to roll right up to the ground-bat's hairy little feet. His nose twitched with excitement.

He pounced (or stumbled) on to the eggs and picked them up, running his quick hungry fingers over their surface. In a rare moment of self-preservation, the baby goblins had decided to snap their eggshells shut. The ground-bat had absolutely no idea what they were but, thinking it

was his best chance of a meal of any kind,
popped one whole egg into his mouth.

Too big! *Far* too big!

For a moment he was stuck. A squeak of
panic and, trying not to choke, he managed
to prise the egg out. Still excited by having
caught something that hadn't tried to eat him
(*always* the worry for any ground-bat), he
decided to scuttle off home and have another go,

but this time with a knife and fork. He picked the eggs up with some difficulty and started to zigzag his way … he knew not where.

Rumble-Bark

Two-Conks, Butterfingers, Mildew and
Drips had gone for a walk. That is to say,
Two-Conks had taken the three Tree Goblins to
see Rumble-Bark, a small, crooked tree of
advancing years. No one knew for sure, but
Two-Conks guessed she was nearly a thousand
years old!

They came upon her sitting, eyes closed, in a
small glade. Having found a spot where the
morning sun was happy to share its warmth,
Rumble-Bark was drinking it in from every one
of her bare and knotted branches.

"Hello there, Two-Conks, nice to see you again

– must be five years since our leaves have crossed!"

"More like ten years is my guess," said Two-Conks (a few years here or there is not so important to a tree).

"Ah, maybe. Whatever which way, it was a time when I had leaves to be crossed!" she

chuckled, her tired old eyes still closed.

"I was wondering—" began Two-Conks.

"I know what you are wondering," said Rumble-Bark. "I may be a little crumpled round the edges, but I can still read a leaf!"

"Oh, I know," said Two-Conks. "I wasn't ..."

"Don't you worry, my dear, I'm only messing with you! It's the cold, is all – makes me a little cranky. Autumn's not a good time for me. It's the winds you see – they strip me of the few leaves I have and, well ... you know." Her eyes were open now and, despite their age, twinkled the colour of golden corn.

She spotted the Tree Goblins. "Oh, there you are, me dears. If I'd known you were here I wouldn't have gone on about me aches and me pains!

"That rotten wood owl you're after wouldn't leave me alone for a minute when it first came into these woods, not two weeks since. It chased away my Tree Goblins and used me for its roostings. I still saw it off, mind!"

She stretched out a creaking branch and pointed west. "As I just told your delightful leaves, Two-Conks, I saw the wretched bird not an hour ago carrying your eggs, me dears. But if it helps at all, they were in the best of spirits, your little ones – singing and shouting and all. It was the wood owl that was looking all of a to-do!"

"Oh, *thank you*!" said Butterfingers and Mildew. "Thank you so much!"

"Nothing to thank me for. Now you go over that there ridge," she said, pointing, "and you'll come across an old wall from who knows what. That wood owl goes there for his sleeps – I'll bet my bark you'll find them there, so don't hang about, Two-Conks."

The Tree Goblins thanked Rumble-Bark with a wave and Two-Conks hurried, in the best way any tree can do such a thing, in the direction of the wall.

Behind them, Rumble-Bark closed her eyes again. The sun was getting warmer. She sighed, stretched out her roots and smiled a long summer's-day smile.

Snootle-Pig

If a bit of luck comes your way, it really is a good idea to make sure you keep hold of it. But the ground-bat wasn't very good at keeping hold of anything.

The Tree-Goblin eggs, for example, were proving very difficult to carry. They weren't heavy, but they kept moving about. And, if the moving wasn't bad enough, the ground-bat found the *talking* most off-putting! They seemed to be arguing – something about the difference between an egg-head and an egg-leg.

He had been in the same spot now for a while and he was keen to leg it away as fast as his silly furry feet could manage it.

He tried a number of different ways of carrying the eggs, but he still kept walking into things. He walked into everything – from boulders, to trees that moved, and tree that *didn't* move.

After another fifteen frantic minutes he sat, panting and exhausted, not five steps from where he had first found the eggs. He was beginning to panic. He had just caught the smell of a snootle-pig's droppings.

At another time, the ground-bat might have settled for the droppings as a last-chance meal before going to bed, but right now they were a lot fresher than he liked. In fact, they were so fresh, he was a little worried that the droppings and the snootle-pig had only just said their goodbyes.

He took a deep breath, picked up the eggs again as best he could, turned and ran straight into the trotters of a *you know what*, scattering the eggs around him.

The ground-bat blinked his tiny sightless eyes and reached out. He ran nervous fingers along the wet rim of a very dribbly nostril. The hair on the back of his ears prickled.

He stuck two fingers up
the nostrils and
drew imaginary
circles, he
wasn't sure
why. Yep,
he thought,
that'll be a
snootle-pig.
Just my luck.

He closed his
tiny eyes and
squeaked as the hot breath
from the snootle-pig's mouth enclosed him like
foul mist. One thing was for sure, he thought
miserably – most things in this rotten wood like
nothing better than to make a chewy and pulpy

mess of ground-bats. It just wasn't fair.

But every now and then even ground-bats can have a bit of luck. The snootle-pig wasn't *that* hungry. Unlike the hapless ground-bat, snootle-pigs are excellent hunters. And, of course, they can, and do, eat any number of ground-bats whenever they like – they're that easy to catch.

Tree-Goblin eggs, however, were a different matter. It was most unusual to find such interesting food just lying around on the woodland floor. And finding three in the arms of a ground-bat was extraordinary.

The snootle-pig, completely ignoring the ground-bat, took the egglets from the unresisting creature and trotted off to bury them somewhere for later.

As he left he accidentally trod on the ground-bat, pushing him face down into his freshly laid droppings.

"Thank you," muffled the ground-bat, "Thank you *so much!*"

And he meant it.

The Clue is in the "Doo-doo"

Butterfingers and Mildew were leaning against Two-Conks, looking with interest at what Drips was doing. He was on his hands and knees, poking his fingers into some snootle-pig droppings.

He sat back on his heels, rolled the droppings around in his fingers, picking off pea-sized balls and popping them into his mouth.

"Hmmm, still warm. Not more than ten minutes is my guess!"

"What's wrong with a nice tray of baked caterpillar bunions?" muttered Mildew.

"Quite," said Butterfingers.

Two-Conks had found the spot where the wood owl had dropped the eggs – a young beech tree had seen her do it – and they were now hot on the tracks of the ground-bat.

At first they'd been confused by the clumsy set of footprints that appeared to go round in circles, sometimes stopping abruptly at one large object or other.

"Cunning little devil, this ground-bat," said Drips with admiration. He had always assumed they were as dumb as they looked. But this one had managed to confuse his trackers.

"Look, see there," Drips said, pointing at an old stump the ground-bat had smashed into, loosening a tooth in the impact. "He's deliberately left a bit of chipped tooth here – trying to show how completely rubbish he is at walking in a straight line. He's pretending he's an idiot and not worth the eating. How clever!"

"But is it the *right* ground-bat – has he got our eggs?" asked Butterfingers.

"Course he's got our eggs, acorn-brains!" snapped Mildew. The strain of the chase was beginning to show.

"Mildew's right," said Drips, "these tracks are quite deep. He must have been carrying something heavier than he was used to. This is the fella – I can feel it in my knee-caps."

"Yes, but can you be really *sure*? If we don't have the right ground-bat we could be losing time – there are more of these little pests running around these woods than anything else."

Two-Conks, who had been listening, leaned down. "It's him all right. Just heard it from the leaves – only, looks like he met a snootle-pig."

Butterfingers groaned.

"Ahh! My babies have been eaten by a snootle-pig!" wailed Mildew.

"I don't think so," said Two-Conks. "It didn't eat the ground-bat; it just took the eggs. My bet is he wasn't hungry, or else the ground-bat would have been eaten. No, I think the snootle-pig had already fed. He's taken the eggs and buried them for later."

"Ahh! My babies have been buried

by a snootle-pig!" screeched Mildew.

"You're right, Conks!" said Drips. "Look!"
He held up a piece of snootle-pig dropping. It
was the *exact* shape of a ground-bat. "What do
you make of this?"

"Ahh! My babies have been
eaten by a ground-bat,
buried by a
snootle-pig, and
now——" Mildew
stopped wailing and
frowned. "Er …"

"Hello," said the
ground-bat, as
politely as possible.
"I'm very pleased to
make your acquaintance!"

"Likewise, I'm sure," replied
Butterfingers. "You don't happen
to remember seeing three
goblin eggs lying
around these parts?"

The ground-bat
blinked and tried
very hard to sound
cheerful. It wasn't easy.
In fact, although he couldn't
see, he felt that he didn't like the
way the large female goblin was
looking at him one little bit.

Oh *great*, he thought. I manage to escape the
jaws of a snootle-pig, only to be the soft inside
bit of Tree-Goblin sandwich. He swallowed. Oh
well, sink or swim – here goes …

Gone but not Forgotten

The snootle-pig had no sooner buried the three goblin eggs when, in the last remaining seconds of his short-term memory, he thought about the eggs again and licked his lips. Perhaps he would eat them now after all.

Snootle-pigs have *terrible* memories. They may be the most feared creature of the wood, but ask them to climb a tree and in five minutes they'll be scratching their heads and wondering how on earth they managed to get up so high. (Funnily enough, they're quite good at climbing.)

The snootle-pig turned round, not having taken ten paces from where he'd buried the eggs, and frowned. They were definitely here *somewhere*, he thought. He stuck his snout among the leaves and, rather like a hoover, noisily searched the ground.

But of course the longer he searched, the dimmer the memory, until … he knew he was searching for something to eat, he was pretty sure about that part, only he wasn't altogether sure *exactly* what it was he was looking for. And the longer he sniffed the more he forgot, until he looked up and wondered what he was doing sniffing a bunch of leaves in daylight. He yawned and trotted off home.

In the wrong direction.

Two-Conks and the three Tree Goblins listened quietly to the ground-bat, who was surprised still

to be alive. Mildew's sobbing had made it
difficult to keep cheerful, but everyone seemed to
believe his tale, and as soon as he'd pointed in
the direction the snootle-pig had taken (he was
guessing of course) they let him go.

He was so happy he ran off with a hop, a skip and a jump … and landed heavily against a rock. He woke up two days later and thought he'd dreamed the whole adventure.

Chapter Thirteen

Quiet before the Storm

The rain fell so suddenly and with such force that for a few moments everything was still in Wandering Wood, even the trees. There was a feeling that such rain could not last. But it did, and for the rest of the day.

The Tree Goblins nestled in the arms of Two-Conks, sheltered from the worst of the rain. Here they were close to the great tree's chest, where his slow wooden heart beat its comforting rhythm.

Drips, remembering his manners, offered the others a drink. All three sat with the sock on their laps.

At first Butterfingers and Mildew thought it would be just as easy to make a leaf-cup, hold it out in the rain and drink from that. But Drips insisted they try, and they were surprised to find it tasted like … bin juice. Yumsk! They drank in silence, content to rest their worried minds, if only for a moment.

75

"The longer you leave it," Drips said, "the better it gets – you really can't beat an old soggy sock. None of this freshwater nonsense. This stuff will curl the very hairs on the end of your tongue!"

Butterfingers had to agree. His eyes were watering, but he couldn't tell if it was rain or tears. He was unable to speak for a minute.

"Now what?" said Mildew miserably. "How are we going to find my babies – my poor little ones, buried like nuts by a snootle-pig!"

The three Tree-Goblin eggs were closer than Mildew thought. Indeed, they were in the very ground where Two-Conks was curling his roots. The egglets, meanwhile, were busy burrowing their way to the surface. They had quite liked being underground, but it was soggy now and the rain was filling their shells, so they decided to see what else they could do in the woods.

When the last of them was tugged free by the other two, without looking up (why would they?) they scampered off, kicking and throwing leaves at each other. The rain drowned out their giggles and they were neither seen nor heard from above.

Of course the three egglets were unaware of the dangers within the wood. Snootle-pigs were just a funny smell to them. If they had seen one, it might have made them think twice about running around in the open.

Ground-bats were less of a problem. The egglets thumped into more than one of them as they played, sending them reeling, like skittles, in all directions.

They were so busy having fun that they didn't notice a long sharp shadow rippling over the fallen leaves towards them. The heavy clouds hadn't yet finished with their rain, but some shadows have no need of sunlight.

The next thing the egglets knew, they were roughly scooped up along with a handful of leaves. Imprisoned between knotted fingers, they heard the rasp of a voice scratch out the words: "GOT YOU!"

Chapter Fourteen

The Storm Monster!

T hunder and lightning don't always dance together, and this evening (already another night was creeping in) the thunder was elsewhere, doing loud things to very different creatures. It's the way things are in this place.

In the flash of lightning Mildew saw her eggs – and she saw a figure scoop them up, all in the blink of an eye, before the darkness spread its cloak again. She wondered if she was dreaming.

"What was that?" she said, sitting up. "Did you see that?"

"Thwwupp?" said Butterfingers. He had a mouthful of sock.

"I saw them, I know I did, my babies, over there – with a terrible monster!"

Two-Conks uncurled his roots and, without hesitating, he made for where Mildew was pointing. Another flash of lightning lit their way.

"THERE, OVER THERE – IT'S THEM! OH, QUICK, TWO-CONKS, HURRY! – BEFORE IT'S TOO LATE!" screamed Mildew.

"I see them!" said Two-Conks, his whole body creaking with the strain as he crashed his way past slumbering trees.

"They're being *eaten* by a *beast* – oh, *please* hurry!"

Drips was a plonk when it came to all things 'sock.' But he was also very brave. He scrambled frantically along Two-Conks, hopping from branch to branch. As Two-Conks drew closer to the beast, so Drips was positioning himself. He suddenly star-jumped into the air, gliding like a flying squirrel.

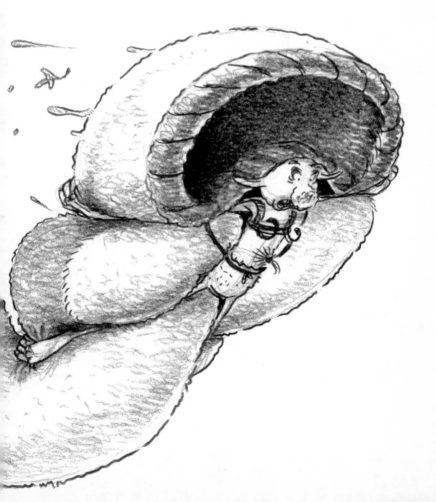

But almost at once his sock ballooned like a parachute, which quite ruined the surprise attack he was after.

He floated gently down towards the creature. A little disappointed, Drips frowned, then took a deep breath.

"AAAAIIIIIIIIII-EEEEEEEEE!!"

His squeal was the squeal of nightmares – it was enough to blow the eyebrows off a snootle-pig.

But the storm was all around them now and the thunder had come back to play with the lightning!

A deafening **crash** just at
that moment was enough
to drown out the cry
from Drips. The dark
figure sat crooked and
curled, broken almost. Its
hands, claw-like, seemed
to be playing with the
eggs, rolling them
around like marbles.
Drips landed
on the back of
the figure
just as the
lightning lit
up the wood
again.

83

Drips screamed, Butterfingers and Mildew screamed, Two-Conks screamed and so did …

In that brief moment of terror the rain stopped, as if the shock of it all had made it do so. Now, in darkness again, there was complete silence.

The egglets were the first to say something. "*Mum?*" Mildew whimpered at the sound of her babies, and fainted.

Butterfingers caught her. But he was so surprised by what he'd done … he dropped her.

Drips swallowed and looked into the very yellow eyes of …

"*Rumble-Bark?*" asked Two-Conks.

"Oh my goodness," said Rumble-Bark, "you've quite given me the shivers, making me jump like that!" She turned around stiffly. Smiling, she held out a branch to Mildew, unlocking her fingers.

"I believe these little tinkers are yours, missy!"

"Mummy!" squealed the egglets and leaped on to Mildew. She groaned and sat up, rubbing her eyes in disbelief.

"MY BABIES!" she cried, and hugged them again and again and again.

"I saw these little ones," said Rumble-Bark, "at the same time as I saw a snootle-pig. It had caught their scent and was tracking them, so I had to grab them before he

did – sorry if it came as a bit of a shock!"

"No, no, not at all," said Butterfingers, picking himself off the ground and brushing himself down. "How can we ever thank you?"

Two-Conks helped Rumble-Bark back on to her roots with a cuddle.

"Ever since we spoke I've been on the look out," said Rumble-Bark. "Happened to *me* once, a long time ago, with a couple of acorns. I know how it feels. Big strong oaks now of course," she chuckled, "but a worry at the time."

"Thanks," said Two-Conks. "We can always rely on you!" Rumble-Bark smiled and leaned closer to Two-Conks. At last, a glint of sunlight had nudged itself through the clouds.

"Um, by the way," she said, pointing, "what *is* that goblin doing with that sock?"

Egg and Sock Race

After the egglets had been given a lesson in knowing what to do if they got lost in the woods again (ask a leaf the way home), Rumble-Bark suggested they celebrate with an egg and spoon race.

"It's what we did when I was just a sapling!" she said.

But no one was quite sure what a spoon was, and Rumble-Bark couldn't remember. After all, what would a goblin possibly want with a spoon when they have fingers and toes that do the job just as well? So Drips suggested using his sock. Why not!

It took two days to find their own socks, one for each team.

With the sun shining again, Two-Conks and Rumble-Bark linked branches and set out a course for the Tree Goblins.

There were Butterfingers and Mildew, of course, against Drips and the egglets. No one knew all the rules, and they couldn't agree on the few they had, so they decided to make them up as they played. There was some winning, some losing, a lot of shouting, and a little throwing.

The race was abandoned after lap three, when Butterfingers slipped and dropped Mildew. She sulked and refused to talk to him for a week.

Despite this chaos, the Egg and Sock Race went on to become a favourite amongst all Tree Goblins, and was a regular activity for many years to come. Some rules were finally agreed, but unfortunately none survive today, so we can only guess how the game was really played.

There are a few clues, however. I recently came across a thin strip of bark, one moonlit walk in the strangest of woods. It was attached to a small wooden post by the slow-drying juices of a foot slug (don't ask). On it were scratched the following words:

HUNT THE EGG.

ALWAYS FOLLOW THE SIGNS, BUT DON'T EAT THEM. CARRY YOUR SOCK AT ALL TIMES – IN YOUR HANDS, NOT YOUR EARS. BEWARE OF THE HOOTER SCOOTER. AND REMEMBER, IF YOU DON'T WANT TO SMELL LIKE A LUMP OF CHEESE ALL YOUR LIFE, NEVER EVER EVER SCRATCH YOUR ...

It stops here. One can only guess what it might have said!

Unfortunately, this makes little sense. And so, with that in mind, I shall leave you, and this story, with my view of what the Tree Goblins' Egg and Sock Race might look like.

Feel free to make up your own rules. And if any of them don't fit, make up some more! Don't forget, rules are made for breaking – ask any goblin. So, help yourself.

Afterword

Nothing is as it seems.

Have you ever taken an early morning stroll in the woods and marvelled at the beautiful singing that our birds spend their day sharing with us?

Well, I'm sorry to say that what you and I believe to be happy tunes are nothing more than squawks of protest. The birds are shooed out of the trees every morning, by the Tree Goblins of course, who need to plump up the leaves after a busy night, ready for the day ahead.

And now that you know this and you listen afresh to these scratchy notes of protest, don't forget the leaves. They could be scuttling past you, carrying important messages to others in the wood.

Possibly, something about you …

Drip's Guide to Sock-Soaking

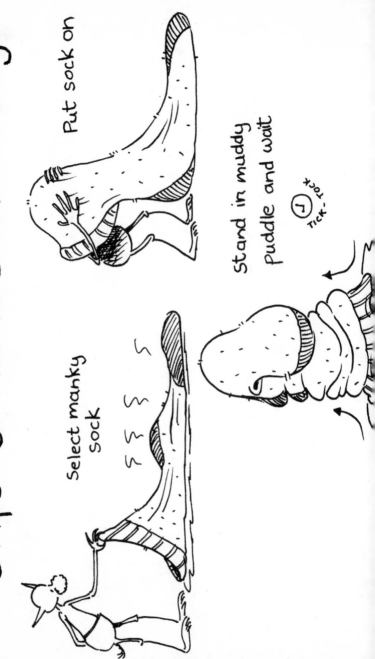

Select manky Sock

Put sock on

Stand in muddy puddle and wait

TICK-TOCK

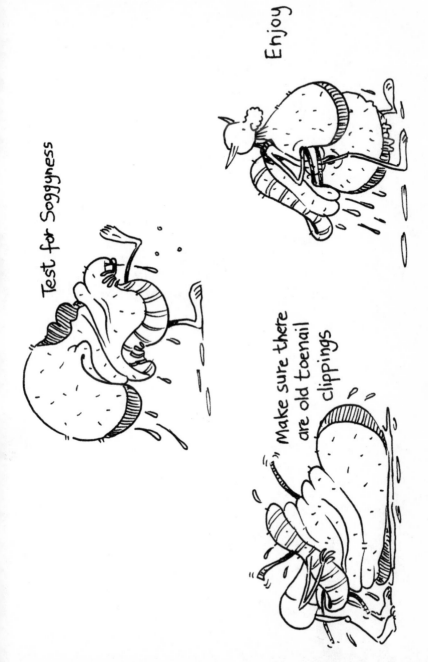